LES MISÉRABLES

VICTOR HUGO

T0333012

LEVEL
4

RETOLD BY KATE WILLIAMS
ILLUSTRATED BY GIORGIO BACCHIN
SERIES EDITOR: SORREL PITTS

PENGUIN BOOKS

UK | USA | Canada | Ireland | Australia
India | New Zealand | South Africa

Penguin Books is part of the Penguin Random House group of companies
whose addresses can be found at global.penguinrandomhouse.com.
www.penguin.co.uk www.puffin.co.uk www.ladybird.co.uk

Penguin Readers edition of *Les Misérables* published by Penguin Books Ltd, 2024
001

Original text written by Victor Hugo
Text for Penguin Readers edition adapted by Kate Williams
Text for Penguin Readers edition copyright © Penguin Books Ltd, 2024
Illustrated by Giorgio Bacchin
Illustrations copyright © Penguin Books Ltd, 2024
Cover illustration by Emile Bayard © Maison de Victor Hugo, Paris/AKG-images
Design project management by Dynamo Limited

Printed and bound in Great Britain by Clays Ltd, Elcograf S.p.A.

The authorized representative in the EEA is Penguin Random House Ireland,
Morrison Chambers, 32 Nassau Street, Dublin D02 YH68

A CIP catalogue record for this book is available from the British Library

ISBN: 978-0-241-63684-8

All correspondence to:
Penguin Books
Penguin Random House Children's
One Embassy Gardens, 8 Viaduct Gardens,
London SW11 7BW

Contents

People in the story

Jean Valjean

Fantine

Cosette

Monsieur and
Madame Thénardier

Javert

Marius Pontmercy

New words

candlesticks

cannon

carriage

cart

coin

rope

Note about the story

Victor Hugo (1802–1885) was a French writer and *Les Misérables* (1862) is his most famous book. In English, *Les Misérables* means "**miserable*** people" but the title of the book has almost always been kept in French.

For hundreds of years, the **rulers** of France were kings, but by the late 1700s many people were poor and hated their rich kings. During the French **Revolution** (1789–1799), King Louis XVI was killed and Napoleon became the ruler of France.

The story of *Les Misérables* begins in 1815, when Napoleon famously lost the Battle of Waterloo, where French soldiers fought against English and other European soldiers. After this, Louis XVIII became King of France, but many French people were still poor and did not want another king. The story ends in 1832, when there was another, smaller revolution. During the night of 5–6 June 1832, **barricades** were built in the narrow streets in the centre of Paris by the **revolutionaries** who were fighting French soldiers.

In French, *Monsieur* means Mr or Sir, and *Madame* means Mrs. Francs were French money that was used until 2002.

Before-reading question

1 Choose three of the characters from the "People in the story" on page 4. What are they like, do you think? For example, are they rich or poor, happy or unhappy, good or bad?

*Definitions of words in **bold** can be found in the glossary on pages 78–80.

CHAPTER ONE

The silver candlesticks

It was 1815 and Monsieur Charles Myriel was the **Bishop** of Digne. He was a kind man, aged about 75, who lived **simply** in a small house. When Monsieur Myriel arrived in Digne, he moved into the bishop's **palace**, next to the hospital. But, as soon as he visited the hospital, he noticed how small it was.

"The bishop's palace is much bigger," he said to the **director** of the hospital. "And there are only three of us living there – myself, my sister and our **servant**. We don't need all those large rooms. You should move the hospital to the palace and we'll live here."

The director agreed and the bishop moved house the next day. His furniture was very old and the only expensive things that he owned were his grandmother's **silver** forks and spoons, and two large silver candlesticks. Monsieur Myriel gave most of his money to the poor. He walked many miles every week to visit the villages around Digne. He was always happy and often laughed like a schoolboy. When he could, he worked in his garden, growing vegetables, fruit and flowers. At night, he often sat in his little garden, looking at the moon, and he felt thankful.

One evening in October 1815, a **stranger** arrived in Digne on foot, and everyone who saw him felt afraid. He was a tall, strong man of about 46, with old, dirty clothes, very short hair and a long beard. No one knew who he was or where he came from.

First, the stranger went into the town hall to show his papers. Fifteen minutes later, he came out and went into the **inn**.

"What would you like, Monsieur?" asked the **landlord**, without looking up.

"Dinner and a bed," replied the man.

"Of course," answered the landlord, and then he looked up. He **stared** at the stranger's dirty clothes and added, "If you can pay."

"I have money," said the man, who went to sit down.

The landlord said something quietly to the kitchen boy, who ran off to the town hall. A few minutes later, the boy came back with a message for the landlord.

"I can't give you a room or dinner," the landlord said to the stranger.

"Why not?" the man asked.

"I don't have any rooms or any food," said the landlord.

"That's not true," said the man. "I'm tired and I'm hungry. I'm not leaving."

"I know who you are. Your name is Jean Valjean!" said the landlord. "You must go!"

So the stranger got up and quietly left the inn. He tried the only other inn in Digne, but they also told him to leave. Then, he walked around the streets, knocking on doors, but no one wanted him. Finally, he sat down on a step near the church. "Maybe I'll have to sleep here," he said to himself. Then, he noticed a small house next to the bishop's palace and went up to the door.

Monsieur Myriel was at home with his sister. "There are stories of a dangerous man in town tonight," the bishop's sister was saying. "People are afraid that something terrible will happen. Shouldn't we **lock** our doors?"

At that moment, there was a loud knock.

"Come in," said the bishop, **calmly**.

The door flew open and the stranger entered. The bishop's sister was **terrified**.

"My name is Jean Valjean," the man said, loudly. "I was a **convict**. I've been in prison for nineteen years. I was **released** four days ago and I've walked thirty-six miles. No one will give me food or a bed for the night. Can I stay here?"

"Of course," said Monsieur Myriel.

"Really?" said the man, in great surprise. "But I've been a convict. Everyone else has closed their doors to me because they think that I'm dangerous. I was given five years in prison for stealing bread and another fourteen years for trying to escape four times. Can I really stay with you? I'll pay as much as you want."

"No, I don't want your money," said Monsieur Myriel. "I'm the bishop. Come and sit by the fire, Monsieur. It's very cold tonight. And, sister, please bring some more light."

His sister got the two silver candlesticks from the cupboard, and the servant brought in soup, bread, meat and fruit. Then, they sat at the table and Valjean ate hungrily.

When dinner was finished, the bishop's sister put the silver forks and spoons away in the cupboard. The bishop got up, picked up one candlestick and gave the other to his visitor. "I'll show you to your room, Monsieur," he said.

Valjean fell asleep quickly, but he woke in the middle of the night. After nineteen years of sleeping on a prison floor, the bed was too comfortable. He lay awake in Monsieur Myriel's silent house, unable to sleep. He could not stop thinking about the bishop's **silver**. Suddenly, he got out of bed, took off his shoes and left the room. He went quietly to the dining room, opened the cupboard and took out the silver forks and spoons. Putting them into his bag, he left the house without making a sound.

A few hours later, Monsieur Myriel discovered that

Valjean was gone, and the silver, too. But he did not worry. "We have other forks and spoons," he told his sister, calmly.

They were having breakfast when there was a knock at the door. Outside, three policemen stood holding Valjean by the arms.

"Ah, there you are!" the bishop said to Valjean. "I'm happy to see you, my friend. I also gave you two silver candlesticks to sell. Why didn't you take them with the forks and spoons?"

Valjean stared at the bishop.

"Do you mean that his story is true?" one of the policemen asked Monsieur Myriel.

"Yes," answered the bishop. "He hasn't stolen anything. You may go."

Monsieur Myriel went to get the two silver candlesticks and gave them to Valjean.

"Now go, my friend," said the bishop. "And don't forget that you've promised to use the money to become an **honest** man."

Valjean was shaking. He still could not speak. He could not remember promising the bishop anything.

"Jean Valjean, my brother," Monsieur Myriel continued, "now you're not owned by **evil**, but by good."

Valjean left the town as fast as he could, his head full of **confusing** thoughts. At times he felt angry, then he felt sad. He almost preferred being in prison because there he was **calm**, feeling nothing. At the end of the day, he sat down on the ground behind a tree and looked around himself at the mountains. A little boy of about ten years old was coming along the path, singing and playing with some coins in his hand. As he passed the tree, the boy dropped one of the coins and it fell near Valjean's foot. Valjean put his boot over it.

"My coin please, Monsieur," said the boy.

"What's your name?" said Valjean.

"I'm Petit-Gervais," replied the boy.

"Go away," said Valjean.

"I want my coin!" cried the child. "My silver coin!"

Valjean stared at the child. Then, he got to his feet and shouted, "Get out of here!"

The terrified child quickly ran away.

Valjean did not move. After a while, he suddenly noticed the silver coin on the ground. "What's that?" he said to himself. Then, he remembered the boy, picked up the coin and looked along the path. But he saw no one.

"Petit-Gervais!" he called as loudly as he could.

There was no answer. Valjean began to run along the path, calling the boy's name again and again. But he could not see the boy anywhere. "Oh, what have I done?" Valjean thought, **miserably**. Then, he dropped to his knees and cried for the first time in nineteen years. The bishop's words filled his mind: "You've promised to become an honest man." The words felt like an attack – a terrible fight between good and evil – which Valjean could not understand. He continued to cry for a long time, knowing only that he was now a changed man.

CHAPTER TWO

Fantine looks for work

One spring evening in 1818, a tired young woman walked down the street of Montfermeil, near Paris, carrying a child. Her name was Fantine and she was very beautiful, with hair the colour of sunlight. Three years earlier, at the age of 15, she left her poor village of Montreuil-sur-Mer to look for a better life in Paris. There, she met a rich young man who became the love of her life. But poor Fantine knew little about the world and after two years was left alone with a little daughter. Now, she was going back to her old village of Montreuil-sur-Mer to find work.

"But how can I, an unmarried woman, work with a child?" thought Fantine, miserably.

She reached an old inn called the Sergeant of Waterloo and stopped outside. A mother sat watching her two little girls playing under a huge cart. She was tall and strong, like a soldier's wife.

"You have two lovely children," Fantine said to her.

"Thank you," replied the woman. "I'm Madame Thénardier. My husband and I own this inn."

"I've walked from Paris," Fantine explained. "My husband is dead and I must find work." She put her child down and the little girl ran off to play with the others.

"What's your little one's name?" asked Madame Thénardier.

"Cosette. She's nearly three."

"So is my eldest. Look at them playing so happily together, like sisters!"

Suddenly, Fantine took Madame Thénardier's hand. "Will you look after my child?" she said.

Madame Thénardier looked surprised but did not answer.

"You see, I can't get a job with a child," said Fantine. "You have two beautiful children – you're a good mother. And I'll come back soon. I'll pay you 6 francs a month."

At that moment, a man's voice called from inside the inn. "Seven francs! And six months paid now."

"That's 42 francs," said Madame Thénardier.

"Plus 15 francs for things that we'll need to buy," called her husband.

"I'll pay it," said Fantine. "And, as soon as I have enough money, I'll come back."

The plan was agreed. Fantine stayed the night at the inn and left early the next morning with a very heavy heart.

———

Thankfully, in the months that followed, Fantine never knew how badly her daughter was treated. The letters from the Thénardiers always promised that Cosette was looked after well, but they were really very bad people. Madame Thénardier loved her own daughters, but she hated Cosette, who had to eat under the table with the cat and the dog. Monsieur Thénardier wrote to Fantine asking for more and more money every month, but nothing was ever spent on Cosette.

At first, Fantine was luckier than her daughter. The little town of Montreuil-sur-Mer was doing very well, thanks to one man, who was now the **mayor**. A few years earlier, at the end of 1815, Monsieur Madeleine arrived in the town with no more than a bag. He started a **jewellery** factory that grew bigger and bigger. It made him and the town rich.

No one knew much about this man or his past. But the people of Montreuil soon began to like him because he shared what he had with the town. They noticed how sad he was when the old Bishop of Digne died. They said, "Maybe Mayor Madeleine comes from Digne."

There was only one man in Montreuil who did not like Mayor Madeleine – a policeman named Javert. Long ago, Javert worked in a prison in Toulon and he had a strange feeling about Mayor Madeleine. He thought that he remembered him being a convict there.

One day, Javert saw an old man named Fauchelevent knocked down in the street by a cart. Mayor Madeleine was trying to help.

"Quick!" cried the mayor. "We must **lift** the cart up or Fauchelevent will die!"

"I only know of one man in France who is strong enough to lift something so heavy," said Javert, staring at the mayor. "He was a convict in Toulon."

The mayor stared back at Javert.

"Help me!" cried Fauchelevent.

The mayor suddenly threw himself to the ground and lifted up the cart. The old man was saved.

As Mayor Madeleine got back on his feet, Javert continued to stare at him.

———

Fantine found a job in the mayor's jewellery factory and rented a small room. For a short while, she was happy. She told no one about her child, but she never stopped thinking about Cosette, and seeing her again. Fantine did not know how to write, so she paid someone in the town to write her letters to the Thénardiers. Then, people at the factory began to talk. They liked nothing better than talking. In the end, they learned from the letter-writer that Fantine had a child but she was never married. The factory director ordered her to leave.

Without work, Fantine's hope was gone. She could not pay for her room and she could not pay the Thénardiers. And now everyone knew about her past. She tried to get work as a servant but no one wanted her. She began to make shirts for soldiers, but the work was very badly paid.

In the winter, Monsieur Thénardier wrote to ask for more money to buy Cosette warm clothes. That evening, Fantine went to the barber's shop and showed him her beautiful blonde hair.

"I'll give you 10 francs for it," said the barber.

"Cut it off," she replied.

She bought a warm dress and sent it to Montfermeil.

But the Thénardiers were very angry not to receive money and gave the dress to their eldest daughter, Éponine. Of course, Fantine did not know this. "My child isn't cold now," the poor woman thought.

As soon as her beautiful hair was gone, Fantine began to hate everyone, most of all Mayor Madeleine, the owner of the jewellery factory. Then, one day, she received a **terrifying** letter. "Cosette is very sick," Monsieur Thénardier wrote. "She needs expensive medicine. If you don't send 40 francs now, she'll die."

Fantine ran into the street with the letter, crying, "It's impossible! How can someone as poor as me pay 40 francs?"

A man heard her. "You have pretty teeth," he said. "I'll give you 40 francs for the two top ones."

"How horrible!" said Fantine, and she went home. But there she read the letter again and thought about her sick daughter. "Without the medicine, Cosette will die," Fantine thought. She hurried back to the man and sold him her two top teeth.

The next day, Fantine sent the 40 francs to the Thénardiers. But it was another terrible lie – Cosette was not ill.

After this, Fantine made shirts for seventeen hours a day, but she still did not have enough money to pay for her room. The next time a letter came from the Thénardiers, she could think of only one more thing to sell – herself. She became a woman of the streets.

CHAPTER THREE

Valjean escapes from Javert

On a cold, snowy evening in the winter of 1823, a woman was walking up and down the street outside the soldiers' café. Her face was white and she looked very sick. A young man began to laugh at her.

"What an ugly woman!" he said as she passed him. "Where are your teeth?"

Fantine did not look at him and walked away. The young man picked up some snow and threw it at her back. She turned and jumped on him, screaming. Hearing the noise, some soldiers came out of the café to watch. Then, a tall man in a black coat appeared through the crowd and took hold of Fantine's arms. "Come with me!" he ordered. It was the policeman Javert.

Javert took Fantine to the police station and sent for Mayor Madeleine.

"You'll go to prison for six months for attacking that man," Javert said.

"No!" cried Fantine. "What about my daughter? If I go to prison, she'll die!" She began to cry wildly and then turned white, almost unable to **breathe**.

Just then a man entered and Javert took off his hat. "Good evening, Mayor," he said.

Fantine stared at him. "Ah, so you're the mayor! All my troubles started because of you! I lost my job at your factory and I needed money to send to my daughter. I didn't want to be a bad woman, but what else could I do?" she said. And, before anyone could stop her, she hit him in the face.

Mayor Madeleine looked at her calmly. "Monsieur Javert, release this woman," he said.

For a moment, neither Javert nor Fantine spoke. They could not believe what they were hearing. Then, Fantine turned to Javert. "Thank you for releasing me," she said to him, and walked towards the door.

"Stop!" called Javert. "Who says that you can go?"

"I do," said the mayor. "I saw what happened earlier. It was the man who did wrong."

Javert tried to **argue**, but it was no use.

"This woman is very ill. She must not go to prison," ordered the mayor.

So Javert left. When Javert was gone, the mayor said to Fantine, "I knew nothing about you losing your job. Why didn't you come to me? I'll give you money. I'll send for your child. I'll look after you both."

"Cosette will be with me again!" thought Fantine. She stared at this strange man and then fell in a **faint** in front of him.

Mayor Madeleine carried Fantine to the hospital and visited her every day. He also sent 300 francs to Thénardier and asked him to bring Cosette to Montreuil. But Thénardier was clever. "If I keep Cosette, this man might send me more money," he thought. And he was right. The mayor sent another 300 francs, but Thénardier still did not send Cosette.

Fantine became sicker and sicker. She kept asking for her daughter. "I'll go and get her tomorrow," Mayor Madeleine promised.

"I'll see her the day after," Fantine thought, happily.

The next morning, as the mayor was getting ready for his journey, Javert came into his office, looking worried.

"What's the matter?" asked the mayor.

"I must leave the police because I've made a terrible mistake," answered Javert. "I wrote to the Director of Police in Paris about you. Many years ago, I worked at the prison in Toulon. There was a convict there called Jean Valjean. When this man was released, he stole from a bishop and also from a little boy. The police want him and I thought that man was you."

The mayor went white.

"But I was wrong," continued Javert. "The Director of Police says that they've found the real Jean Valjean and his trial is in Arras tomorrow. So I cannot continue being a policeman."

"No, you're an honest man, Javert. You must stay," said the mayor.

After this, the mayor's mind was full of confusing thoughts. "I should be happy. Javert has his Jean Valjean and I can do good here in Montreuil. What will happen to the town without me?" But the mayor was not happy. "That man in Arras isn't Valjean," he thought. "I must go to Arras and put this right." Then, he thought of Fantine. "I've promised to bring her daughter to her. Who will save Cosette if I go to prison?"

Suddenly, he felt that he could hear the bishop's voice saying, "Will you allow an honest man to be sent to prison in your place?" Then, Mayor Madeleine knew that he must go to Arras.

———

When the mayor arrived at the trial in Arras, he **proved** that he was the real Valjean. Everyone looked at him in surprise, but no one did anything. "If the police don't want me now, I'm going," he said. "But you know where to find me."

The next morning, he was at Fantine's side with the doctor when she woke. "Cosette?" she asked, quickly.

"Be calm," said the doctor. "We'll bring her when you're better."

Suddenly, Javert appeared. Fantine was terrified.

"He wants me, not you," the mayor told her.

"Come with me, Jean Valjean!" Javert shouted.

"Wait," said the mayor, quietly. "First, I need to get this woman's child from Montfermeil. Come with me if you want."

"Cosette!" cried Fantine. "Isn't she here?"

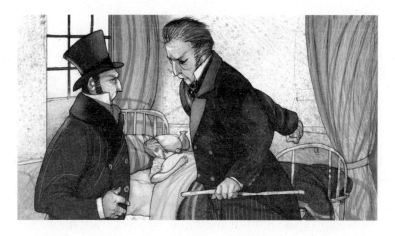

She sat up, her eyes wide open, and tried to speak again. Then, she suddenly fell back, dead.

"Come with me now!" Javert ordered Valjean.

Quickly, Valjean pulled a metal bar from the bed and held it up at Javert.

Then, he turned to Fantine, picked up her hand and kissed it.

"You've killed this woman and now you want her daughter to die, too!" he cried to Javert. "Leave this house right now! Follow me if you must, but you'll need to bring a lot of men."

Javert looked at the metal bar and ran from the room.

Valjean hurried home. He was putting the two silver candlesticks in a bag when he heard the police arrive. He could hear Javert's voice. But when the police entered the house they found no one.

An hour later, Valjean was walking quickly away from Montreuil through the trees, in the direction of Paris.

CHAPTER FOUR
Cosette is saved

Life at the Thénardiers' inn, the Sergeant of Waterloo, was very hard for little Cosette. By now she was only eight years old, but she did all the hard work. All day, she had to wash, clean and carry for Madame Thénardier.

Monsieur Thénardier was no better than his wife. Everyone who came to the inn heard his story about the inn's name. "I was a soldier at the Battle of Waterloo," he told them. "I saved a man's life, you know." But this was just another of his lies. Thénardier was only at Waterloo that terrible night in 1815 to steal from the dead bodies of soldiers.

After the battle, he was pulling a ring from a dead soldier's finger when the man suddenly opened his eyes and spoke.

"Thank you for saving my life," he said, quietly. "Who are you?"

"Thénardier, a French soldier like you."

"Thank you, Thénardier. There's money inside my jacket – please take it."

But this money was already safely inside Thénardier's coat.

Thénardier looked in the soldier's jacket and said, "Someone has stolen your money. I've saved your life and now I must go."

"I shan't forget your name, Thénardier. And please remember mine – it's Georges Pontmercy."

Later, Thénardier did remember Pontmercy. He painted a picture of himself, the brave soldier, carrying Pontmercy on his back at the Battle of Waterloo. He gave his inn its new name and put this picture on the wall.

———————

One very cold winter's evening, Madame Thénardier sent Cosette out to get water. It was very dark, but Cosette knew the way well. She filled her bucket with water and began to carry it home. It was a long way and the bucket was very heavy. She wanted to cry, but she was afraid that Madame Thénardier might see her. The poor little girl felt that she was everywhere. So Cosette bravely hurried on.

Suddenly, a tall, strong man was walking at her side. "That looks like a very heavy bucket, my child," he said. "I'll carry it for you."

He took the bucket and asked her name. When she told him, he stopped and looked at her.

"Who has sent you out to get water so late at night?" he asked.

"Madame Thénardier, the innkeeper's wife. Please give me the bucket when we get there or she'll hit me."

"That's where I'm staying tonight," said the man.

When Cosette opened the door of the inn, Madame Thénardier shouted, "You've been a long time!" Then, she saw the stranger with Cosette.

"We have no room, Monsieur," she told him.

"I can sleep on the floor, and I'll still pay for a room," he replied.

"All right," she said.

"Is this child yours?" he asked.

"Oh no! Her mother left her here years ago. But we think that she may be dead because she hasn't replied to our last letter."

Before he left the next morning, the stranger said to Madame Thénardier, "I'm sure that it costs you a lot to look after that child. Why don't I take her away?"

At that moment, Monsieur Thénardier appeared. "But we love that little girl," he said. "She's like a daughter to us. And I don't even know your name."

"If I take her, I will not tell you my name or where I live. You'll never see her again. Do you agree? Yes or no?"

Thénardier thought for a moment. "I must have 1,500 francs," he said.

The stranger took out the money and held it up. "Bring Cosette now," he said.

A short while later, he and the girl began their journey to Paris, walking together hand in hand. And feeling her small hand in his, for the first time that he could remember, Valjean felt love.

———

For weeks, they lived happily in a poor little apartment in Paris, where Cosette laughed and sang from the moment she awoke. Watching her play and teaching her to read were the only things in Valjean's life that he cared about. She called him Father and knew him by no other name. These two friendless people each had someone to love.

Valjean felt safe from Javert, but he still chose not to go out in the day. Their old landlady did all the shopping and cooking. In the evenings, Valjean and Cosette went for walks in the quiet streets near their building.

But one night, when Cosette was in bed, Valjean thought that he heard someone outside their door. He listened carefully. Then, he put his eye to the keyhole and looked through. A tall man in a long black coat was walking away. "Could it be Javert?" thought Valjean.

The next evening, when it was dark, Valjean took Cosette by the hand and they went out for their walk. Valjean looked carefully up and down the streets, but he saw no one. Cosette asked no questions, even when he kept changing direction to check that they were not followed. With him, she felt safe.

But suddenly Valjean saw a policeman **hiding** in the **darkness** at the end of the street. He quickly turned and went another way, but another policeman was hiding there, too. A little light fell on the man's face. It was Javert.

Valjean picked up Cosette and hurried down a narrow street, until they came to a wall. There was only one way out.

"Who's coming after us?" asked Cosette, a little frightened.

"Don't be afraid," Valjean said in her ear. "Madame Thénardier is coming. But you're safe with me. Just do what I say."

Valjean took off his scarf and quickly put it under Cosette's arms. "Stand with your back against the wall while I climb up," he said. Then, he pulled himself up the wall and lay down on top of it. "Now, pass me the ends of the scarf," he told Cosette as he reached down. She felt herself lifted from the ground on to the wall.

Valjean could hear Javert's voice shouting to the other policeman. With Cosette on his back, he made his way along the wall, reached a tree and climbed down to the ground.

They were in a garden and an old man was walking towards them.

"Please help us!" Valjean said, quickly. "I'll give you 100 francs."

"Mayor Madeleine!" said the old man, in surprise. It was Fauchelevent, the old man from Montreuil who fell under the cart years ago.

"What are you doing here?" Valjean asked.

"You got me a job here at this **convent** as a gardener. Don't you remember? But what about you? Have you and the child fallen from the skies?"

"Please help us," said Valjean. "The child is very cold and needs to rest."

Half an hour later, Cosette was asleep by the fire in the gardener's **simple** little house. Fauchelevent brought Valjean bread, cheese and wine.

"No other men are allowed in the convent," he said to Valjean. "But I'll tell the **nuns** that I have a brother who can come to help me with the garden. And the nuns will teach your daughter at the convent school. All will be well. But first you'll need to leave secretly and come back through the front door."

CHAPTER FIVE

Marius falls in love

Many years passed and by 1828 the inn at Montfermeil, the Sergeant of Waterloo, was closed. The Thénardiers were gone.

One day, a young man arrived there, looking for Monsieur Thénardier. "He left years ago. No one knows where that family is," he was told.

"Monsieur Thénardier saved my father's life at Waterloo," the young man replied. "I must find him and thank him!" For the young man's name was Marius Pontmercy and he was Georges Pontmercy's only son.

As a child, Marius knew nothing about his father. He lived near Paris with his grandfather, Monsieur Gillenormand, and only knew that his grandfather hated his father. Monsieur Gillenormand never wanted his daughter to marry the soldier Georges Pontmercy, who fought for Napoleon. Napoleon lost at Waterloo and Monsieur Gillenormand hated him, too.

After Marius's mother died, Monsieur Gillenormand took the little child and never allowed him to see his father. He threw away the loving letters that Pontmercy wrote to his son.

When Marius was 17, he began to study at a college in the centre of Paris. One day, his grandfather said, "Your father is sick and wants to see you." Marius was surprised. He believed that his father was not interested in him, so he did not love him. By the time Marius arrived, his father was dead.

"Your father loved you very much," the old servant told him. "He came to see you in church every month, but he could never speak to you because of your grandfather."

Then, the servant gave Marius a letter. In it was written,

A soldier called Thénardier saved my life at Waterloo. I believe that he was an innkeeper in Montfermeil. If my son ever meets this man, I hope that he will be good to him.

After this, Marius began to love his father with all his heart and learned everything that he could about his life as a soldier. "My father was very brave and now he's dead!" thought Marius, sadly. Then, he went to Montfermeil, looking for Thénardier.

While Marius was gone, his grandfather said to himself, "That young man is keeping a secret, I'm sure. Maybe he's fallen in love!"

He found a letter in Marius's room and was sure that it was a love letter. But it was Georges Pontmercy's letter. Monsieur Gillenormand was very angry and, when Marius came home, they argued.

"If you take Pontmercy's side, and Napoleon's, against our king, you must leave this house," shouted Monsieur Gillenormand.

"Down with the king!" Marius shouted back.

His grandfather turned white. "Get out of this house!" he ordered.

Marius left without knowing where he was going. He had 30 francs and a few clothes in a bag. He arrived in the centre of Paris and still did not know what to do.

Suddenly, he heard a young man call out, "Marius Pontmercy!"

Marius stared at him. "Who are you?" he said.

"My name is Courfeyrac. I study at the same college as you. And these are my friends. Where do you live?"

"Nowhere," answered Marius. "Right now, I have nowhere to go."

"Then come and live with me and my friends," said Courfeyrac, smiling.

———

Courfeyrac and his friends were clever young men with wild ideas about **revolution**. They argued that it was wrong for France to have a king again. Marius was poor and his stomach was often empty, but his head was filled with confusing new ideas. For three years, Marius studied hard, and finally he got a job and a room of his own. He was still very poor but he was pleased that he never borrowed money from anyone. He often thought about his father. "One day, I'll find the brave man that saved his life and I'll be good to him," he promised himself.

Marius was now a handsome young man of 20, with black hair and a thoughtful face. He loved to take long walks in the Luxembourg Gardens, dreaming. He never noticed the young women turning to look at him, until one day he saw a beautiful girl on a seat, next to a white-haired man. Her smile was like sunlight and her voice was like music. Marius passed near the seat and his eyes met hers.

"She's an **angel**," he breathed.

After this, Marius went to the Luxembourg Gardens at the same time every day, and the beautiful young woman was always there with her father. Once, as Marius walked near their seat, they got up and came towards him. His heart was **beating** fast. His angel was coming! As she passed him, the girl lifted her eyes and looked at him sweetly. She was more beautiful than ever.

From that moment, Marius's love grew. He dreamed of his angel every night.

Then, he wanted more. He wanted to know where she lived. So one day he followed her and her father home and watched them go inside a building.

"Did the man from the first floor just come in?" Marius asked the doorman.

"No, the man on the third floor," said the doorman.

Marius looked up at the windows on the third floor, his heart full of love. The next day, he followed the couple home again and this time the father turned to look at him before going inside. After that, they never came to the Luxembourg Gardens again. Marius went to their house, but the windows on the third floor were dark.

"They've moved," the doorman told him. "I don't know where to."

With a terrible pain in his heart, Marius walked home.

CHAPTER SIX

Marius meets his neighbours

Months went by and Marius had only one thought – to see that beautiful face again. He looked everywhere, but it was hopeless.

One dark winter's evening, Marius was walking home sadly to his room. It was in a poor part of Paris, in a large, dirty building. Many of the rooms in this **miserable** building were empty, but Marius knew that a very poor family lived in the room next to his. The father, mother and two daughters shared one cold, dirty room. A few weeks before, after hearing from the cleaner that they could not pay their rent, Marius secretly paid it for them. He knew that their name was Jondrette, but he knew nothing else about them.

As Marius got near his building, two girls turned the corner and ran into him without stopping. As they hurried away, he noticed their shoeless feet and the holes in their clothes.

"Are they running from the police?" Marius thought. Then, he saw a thick grey envelope on the ground. "Maybe those girls dropped it," he thought. "If there's an address inside, I can give it back to them." So he took the envelope up to his room and opened it. Inside, there were four letters. Each letter was addressed to a different person and signed with a different name. But the writing was the same and all the letters asked for money. Marius could not understand it.

Early the next morning, there was a knock at his door. A girl of about 16 stood there. She had no shoes, her hair was dirty, and there were holes in her skirt.

"Here's a letter for you, Monsieur Marius," she said. He was surprised that she knew his name because he did not know her.

He opened the letter and read it.

Dear neighbour,
I learned that you kindly paid my rent a few weeks ago.
Thank you, young man. We haven't eaten for two days
and my wife is sick. Can I hope that you'll be kind to
us again? My daughter can tell you how hungry we are
and she'll wait for your answer.
Jondrette

It was the same writing as the other four letters. Suddenly, Marius understood. The girls that ran into him yesterday were his neighbour's two daughters. "Jondrette writes letters asking people for money and gets his daughters to **deliver** them," thought Marius.

He went to get the envelope and handed it to the girl. "I found this on the street yesterday," he said.

"Oh, thank you! We looked everywhere but couldn't find it," she said. "If we don't deliver the letters, Father is angry with us. But the kind old man will be at St Jacques church now, so I can go and give him his letter!"

"Wait, take this," said Marius, giving her a silver coin. It was his last 5 francs, but he felt sorry for the poor girl.

"You're a true friend!" she cried, and was gone.

Since leaving his grandfather's house, Marius knew what it was like to be poor. But this girl's life was totally different. It was real **misery**. How terrible to see children with no shoes on their feet and with nothing to eat! Marius was angry with himself for not caring more about his neighbours before. He often heard their voices through the wall, but he never usually thought about them.

Later that morning, he was looking at the wall between him and his neighbours when he noticed a hole near the top. He climbed on a chair and looked through the hole into a dark and dirty room, with little furniture and one window. Jondrette was by the fire, and his wife and youngest daughter were lying on the beds.

Suddenly, the door flew open and the eldest daughter ran in.

"He's coming! The kind man from the church is coming!" she cried.

"Wife, put out the fire!" shouted Jondrette.

But his wife did not seem to hear him. So Jondrette threw some water on the fire. Then, he put his foot through the seat of the only chair.

"Get up and break the window!" he shouted at his youngest daughter. She did what he said and when the glass cut her hand she began to cry. Through the broken window, snow was falling.

"It all looks good," Jondrette said, looking around the miserable room. "Now we're ready for him."

At that moment, there was a knock at the door. Jondrette hurried to open it.

"Come in, Monsieur," he cried. "And the young lady, too."

Marius could not believe his eyes. His angel was there, as beautiful as ever!

"We've brought you some clothes," said her father, giving Jondrette a bag.

As Jondrette turned to give the bag to his eldest daughter, Marius could see how angry he was. He wanted money, not clothes.

"Thank you, Monsieur," said Jondrette, turning back to the old man. "You see how poor we are. We have nothing – no money, no food, no fire. It's so cold, but even the window is broken. Our only chair is broken. My wife is sick in bed.

My daughter cut her hand in a machine at work and she might lose her arm! And I must pay a year's rent tomorrow. Sixty francs! If I don't, we'll be out on the streets!"

Marius knew that this was a lie. "I paid their rent myself," he thought.

"Monsieur, I have only 5 francs here," replied the old man. "But I'll bring you 60 francs at six o'clock this evening."

A moment later, the man and his daughter were gone. Marius's only thought was to follow his beautiful angel. He did not want to lose her again. He hurried down the stairs and out to the street, but it was too late. He could not see them anywhere. He went back upstairs to his room, feeling miserable.

Jondrette's eldest daughter was waiting outside his door.

"What do you want?" he asked her, angrily.

"What's the matter, Monsieur Marius?" she replied. "You were kind to me this morning."

"Nothing," he said. Then, an idea came to him. "An old man and his daughter just came to visit you, didn't they? Can you give me their address?"

She looked at him hard. "I don't have the beautiful young lady's address, but I can find it for you. And what will you give me?"

"Anything that you want," replied Marius.

CHAPTER SEVEN
Marius finds Thénardier

Marius fell into a chair, his head full of confusing thoughts.

Suddenly, he heard Jondrette shouting, "It was him, I tell you! I remember his face."

Was Jondrette talking about his angel's father? Marius quickly jumped on to the chair to look through the hole in the wall.

"I've got him now!" Jondrette said to his wife. "And the girl – that's *her*!"

"How can my poor daughters have no shoes while that girl has beautiful clothes?" cried his wife, angrily.

"I have a plan," replied her husband. "He's coming back at six o'clock and we'll get him!" He gave a horrible laugh. "No one will hear. Monsieur Marius will be out. He never comes home before eleven. But we'll need the help of some friends. I'll go and speak to them now and this evening we'll catch him. Tomorrow we'll eat like kings!"

Marius did not understand what Jondrette and his wife were talking about, but he knew that something terrible could happen to his angel and her father. He had to help them.

He left his room, went down to the street without making a sound, and hurried to the police station. There, he told the office boy that he needed to speak to the Director of Police.

"He's not here," said the office boy. "I'll get Monsieur Javert."

Soon, a tall, terrifying man in a long black coat appeared. Marius was frightened of him, but felt sure that this man could help. He told Javert everything and gave him Jondrette's address.

Javert thought hard, then he said, "Are you afraid of this man and his friends?"

"Of course not," answered Marius.

Javert pulled two small guns from his coat and handed them to Marius. "Then take these. Go home and wait quietly in your room. Jondrette must think that you're out. Wait for the men to arrive, and, when you think that it's gone far enough, **fire** the gun once as a sign to me. I'll be waiting in the building."

Marius took the guns and put them in his coat.

At half past five, he was back in his room, waiting in the dark. His heart was beating fast. When he heard Jondrette come home, he climbed silently on to the chair by the wall.

"Is everything ready?" Jondrette said to his wife. "Are you sure that our neighbour is out?"

"Yes," replied his wife. "He hasn't been home all day."

"We should still check," said Jondrette. "Go and look," he ordered his eldest daughter.

Marius just had time to hide under his bed. Very soon, a light appeared at the bottom of his door and the door opened. The eldest daughter came in with a candlestick and looked around her. As the girl stood near the bed, Marius began to shake. He was sure that he was breathing loudly enough for her to hear.

The girl looked in the mirror and began singing a love song quietly to herself.

"What are you doing in there? Come back!" shouted her father from the next room.

The girl had one last look in the mirror and left. After a moment, Marius came out from under the bed and climbed back on to the chair to look through the wall. A bright fire was now burning in the Jondrettes' room and in this fire the end of a metal bar was turning red hot. In the corner of the room, there were a lot of pieces of rope. "What terrible thing have these people planned?" thought Marius, his heart beating wildly.

He carefully took one of the guns from his coat.

There was a knock at the door and his angel's father appeared. "I've brought the 60 francs," he said.

"You're very kind, Monsieur," said Jondrette.

Marius watched, but he was not afraid. The gun was in his hand and the police were somewhere in the building, waiting for his sign.

While Jondrette began to talk about his poor wife and daughters, a man came into the room and sat down on the bed. After a while, three more men came in, one after the other.

"Who are these men?" the old man asked, looking surprised.

"Oh, just neighbours," Jondrette replied. Then, his voice suddenly changed. "Don't you know who I am?" he shouted. "My name is Thénardier. I was the innkeeper at Montfermeil. Remember?"

"No," said the old man, calmly.

Marius's arm dropped to his side. "Thénardier? Can it be true? The man who saved my dear father's life? Have I found him at last?" he thought, miserably. "My father wanted me to help this man, but I'm going to hand him to the police." Marius could not believe it. "But, if I don't act, my angel's father will die. What should I do?"

"You stole the child from me eight years ago! All my troubles since then have been because of you!" Jondrette was shouting at the old man. "But I'm the one who's laughing now because I've got you!"

"You've made a mistake," said the old man, quietly.

At that moment, one of the men from the bed stood up. He had a metal bar in his hand. The old man moved towards the window, but in a second the other three men pulled him away.

Marius had to do something. He lifted the gun and moved his finger. "Father, I'm sorry," he thought. But then Thénardier shouted, "Don't hurt him!" and Marius let his arm fall again.

The old man began to fight his attackers. He knocked one to the floor, but the other three threw him on to the bed and held him there.

"He's strong for an old man!" shouted Thénardier. "**Tie** him to the bed with these ropes."

Then, Thénardier went to get a pen and paper, and ordered the old man to write a letter. "Write this," he said. "*My dear daughter, come immediately. I need you. The person who delivers this message will bring you.*"

The old man did not argue.

"Now, write your address on the front," ordered Thénardier. Then, he took the letter and gave it to his wife. "Deliver this and come back as soon as you can."

"I'll explain what's going to happen," Thénardier said when she was gone. "My wife will put your daughter in a carriage and the driver will take her somewhere safe. Then, my wife will come back here. As soon as you've given me 200,000 francs, I'll send your daughter back to you. But, if you tell the police, your daughter won't be safe any more."

Marius was terrified. Now he could not fire the gun without putting his angel in danger. What could he do?

Everyone waited for Thénardier's wife to come back. Finally, she came running into the room, crying, "It was the wrong address. There was no one there!"

At the same moment, Marius saw the old man jump up, shaking off the ropes. "He cut them while they were waiting!" thought Marius. The old man ran to the fire and picked up the red-hot metal bar.

Then, Javert suddenly appeared at Jondrette's door, unable to wait for Marius's sign any longer. Behind him were fourteen more policemen.

"Where's the poor man that this murderer was attacking?" said Javert.

But the old man was nowhere to be seen. When the police arrived, he quickly left by the window and was already a long way away.

CHAPTER EIGHT
A love letter

For a while after his escape from Thénardier, Valjean was worried. Thénardier was another person that he needed to hide from. First, there was Javert. Then, there was the young man from the Luxembourg Gardens. Valjean could see that Marius was in love with Cosette and that she loved him back. He hated this young stranger who might take his dear child away. When Marius followed them home, Valjean knew that they had to move. He rented a house with a pretty garden and a large gate opening on to Plumet Street. But there was also a secret path to it between two high walls that Valjean always used, which came out a quarter of a mile away. After their move, they stopped visiting the Luxembourg Gardens and he did not even allow Cosette to go into their own garden. She became silent and sad but never questioned him.

But, as soon as Valjean heard that Thénardier was in prison, he felt better. No one was following them, so it was safe for Cosette to go into the garden. They both became calmer and happier.

———

After that terrible evening when the police took Thénardier away, Marius went to live with his friend Courfeyrac again. He did not want to speak to the police or to be at Thénardier's trial. Every week, he sent 5 francs to Thénardier in prison.

For Marius, everything was now misery. The only place that he liked to be was an empty field where he could be alone and think of his love. He was here one morning in spring when a young woman came towards him. It was Thénardier's eldest daughter, Éponine.

"Monsieur Marius, I've found you at last!" she said. "Aren't you pleased to see me? But you look sad."

Marius said nothing.

"I can make you happy," she said. "I have the address of the young lady."

Marius jumped up and took her by the hand. "Tell me! Where is it?" he cried.

"I'll take you there," she said.

"Wait! Promise me that you won't give this address to your father."

"How can I when he's in prison?" she asked.

———————

One evening, a few days later, Cosette left her seat in the garden and walked around. When she came back to the seat, she was surprised to see a large stone there. Under the stone was an envelope, with a long letter inside. She read it quickly, again and again. It was not addressed to anyone or signed, but she knew that it was from the young man from the Luxembourg Gardens. It was all about love.

The next evening, without knowing why, she put on her best dress before going to her seat in the garden. Suddenly, she felt sure that someone was behind her.

She stood up and turned round.

The young man was there.

"I'm sorry. Don't be afraid," he said. "I couldn't bear it any longer. I haven't seen you for so long. You see, you're my angel. I love you!"

She fell down in a faint and he caught her, holding her in his arms. Then, she took his hand and laid it on her heart.

"You love me then?" he asked.

"You know that I do," she answered, softly.

They dropped down to the seat together and kissed. Then, they began to speak of their love, their dreams and their secrets. At the end, she put her head against him and asked, "What's your name?"

"Marius," he said. "And yours?"

"My name is Cosette."

———

From that day, Marius came to the garden every evening. He and Cosette lived in a wonderful dream. Only Éponine knew that he was there.

But, one evening, Marius found Cosette crying.

"My father says that we must leave Paris because trouble is coming. We might go to England," she said.

"Will you go?" asked Marius, coldly.

"I don't want to leave you, but what else can I do?" she asked. "Can't you come, too?"

"How can I go to England? I have no money," said Marius. "Cosette, if you go away, I will die."

She began to cry again.

"I've had an idea," he said, taking her hand. "I'll come the day after tomorrow at nine o'clock. And, if you ever need it, this is my address." He took out his knife and used it to write "16 Verrerie Street" on the wall.

The next day, after four years, Marius went to visit his grandfather. Monsieur Gillenormand was very happy to see his grandson, but he did not show it. He was 91 and frightened of dying without seeing Marius again.

"Why have you come?" he asked.

"Will you allow me to marry?" said Marius.

"Marry?" said his grandfather, with a cold laugh. "At the age of 21? Have you become very rich? Or does the girl that you want to marry have money?"

Marius shook his head.

"What's her name?" asked Monsieur Gillenormand.

"Cosette Fauchelevent."

His grandfather began to laugh wildly. "You want me to agree that you should marry a poor woman when you have nothing? No, never!"

"Oh, Grandfather!" cried Marius, miserably.

This brought a change in Monsieur Gillenormand. "My boy, if you're in love, you'll need some new clothes! I'll give you some money. But you don't need to get married!"

Marius could not believe his ears. "Do not speak about her like that! I'll never ask you for anything again. Goodbye!"

Before Monsieur Gillenormand could say anything else, Marius was gone.

CHAPTER NINE
A bullet is stopped

Marius was in misery. He walked the streets until the early hours of the morning and finally went home to Courfeyrac's place and threw himself on his bed. When he woke up, Courfeyrac was hurrying out.

"Haven't you heard? The new revolution is beginning!" Courfeyrac said, excitedly. "Are you coming to the **barricades**?"

Marius did not know what his friend was talking about. But that evening, before he went to see Cosette, he put Javert's guns in his coat, without knowing why. When he reached the house in Plumet Street, Cosette was not in the garden. The house was in darkness. He ran to the door and knocked loudly, not caring about her father.

"Cosette! Cosette!" he cried.

There was no reply. She was gone. His life was over.

Suddenly, he heard a voice calling, "Monsieur Marius! Your friends are waiting for you at the barricade on Chanvrerie Street."

It sounded like Éponine's voice, but when Marius reached the gate he saw a young man disappearing round the corner of the street.

There was only one place that Marius could go. Without Cosette, he did not want to live and he knew where he could die bravely. He began to walk quickly towards

Chanvrerie Street. There were lots of soldiers about and crowds of poor people, too. A war was coming to these streets, between the people of France. But as Marius got nearer to Chanvrerie Street all the windows were closed and the houses were silent. The sky was black. The city was holding its breath, waiting.

Marius came to the top of Chanvrerie Street. A short way down, he could see the back of the barricade, outside an inn. Men with guns were on their knees, ready to fire. Courfeyrac was there with them.

Marius was frightened, but he had to be strong. He thought about his father fighting bravely in so many wars. "It's my time now to be brave," he thought. He was ready to meet death. "Cosette doesn't love me any more because she has gone without waiting for me," he told himself.

Suddenly, a soldier on the other side of the barricade shouted, "Who goes there?"

"The French Revolution!" called Courfeyrac.

"Fire!" came the answer.

There was a storm of light and noise as the fighting began. Soldiers climbed on to the barricade. Bodies fell. The red flag fell. Marius watched as a boy of about 11 climbed up to put back the flag. At that moment, a soldier pointed his gun at the boy. But, before the soldier could **shoot**, Marius fired one of Javert's guns and hit the soldier, who fell down.

Then, Marius noticed a large barrel of **gunpowder** near the door of the inn. As Marius ran towards it, through the smoke, another soldier pointed a gun at his head. But a hand was quickly laid over the end of the gun from behind, stopping the **bullet**. Marius was not hit.

He reached the barrel of gunpowder and picked it up. "Get back or I'll use this gunpowder to **blow up** the barricade!" he cried, and the soldiers quickly ran off.

Marius went into the smoke-filled inn and everyone stood around him.

"You're here!" cried Courfeyrac.

"You saved my life!" cried the boy, who was called Little Gavroche. "We've already taken a **spy**," he said, pointing at a man tied up with ropes near the wall.

Marius saw that it was Javert, but nothing felt real to him.

"Long live France! Long live the future!" Courfeyrac and his men shouted.

A short while later, Marius went out to check the barricade. As he turned, he heard a very quiet voice. "Monsieur Marius!"

There was someone on the ground with no shoes. "It's me, Éponine. I'm dying!"

She was dressed as a man.

"There's **blood** on your shirt! I'll carry you inside," said Marius. As he got down to pick her up, he saw a hole through her hand.

"I stopped a bullet to save you," she said. "The bullet went through my hand, but it came out through my back. Don't move me. Nothing can save me now. Just sit down next to me."

Marius did what she said and she put her head on his knees. "I feel no pain now," she said. She was silent for a moment and then she said, "Everyone here is going to die. But I wanted to die before you. I was waiting for you to come. Do you remember the day that I came to your room? I was happy that day. And I'm happy now."

Just then, they heard Little Gavroche singing.

"That's my brother. He mustn't see me," Éponine said.

"Your brother?" said Marius, very surprised.

"My parents didn't want him. He lives on the streets and he's happy," she said. She lifted her head and brought her face close to Marius's. Her breathing was very difficult now. "I've got a letter for you in my jacket. Take it. I didn't want to give it to you, but I must. But please promise to kiss me when I'm dead. I shall feel it."

She let her head drop back and closed her eyes. Then, she opened them again and said, "You see, Monsieur Marius, I think that I was a little in love with you."

She tried to smile again, and died.

Marius kept his promise. He placed a kiss on that cold head, a thoughtful goodbye to a poor girl. Then, he opened the letter, his hands shaking. The address on the front was 16 Verrerie Street. It read,

My dearest,
Father says that we must leave today. First, we will go
to 7 Homme-Armé Street. Then, we leave for England.
Cosette

Marius kissed the letter and for a moment he was happy. "Cosette does love me!" he thought. But then he said to himself, "She's going away. Her father's taking her to England and my grandfather doesn't want us to marry. Nothing has changed. I must still die. But, first, there are two things that I need to do – to tell Cosette and to save Gavroche, Thénardier's son and Éponine's brother."

He took a notebook from his jacket and pulled out some paper. On it, he wrote, "I want to marry you, but it's impossible. My grandfather won't allow it and I have no money. I came to your house, but you were already gone. So I must die. I love you." On the front he wrote the address in Cosette's letter.

Then, he opened his notebook again and wrote in it, "My name is Marius Pontmercy. Take my body to my grandfather, Monsieur Gillenormand, 6 Filles-du-Calvaire Street." He put his notebook back in his coat. Then, he called for Gavroche.

"Will you deliver this letter for me?" he asked, when the boy came running.

"But the barricade might fall and I won't be here," said the boy. "Can't I take it tomorrow?"

"No, the soldiers will be back early in the morning and you won't be able to get out. Go now."

Gavroche took the letter. "All right," he said, running off. "If I take the letter quickly, I'll be back in time," he thought.

CHAPTER TEN

At the barricade

Valjean was sitting miserably outside a house in Homme-Armé Street. He could hear the sound of fighting in another part of the city. Paris was full of police and soldiers, and he was afraid that they might find him.

After a while, a small boy appeared through the darkness.

"I have a letter for number 7," the boy said.

"That's my address. Give it to me," replied Valjean.

"But it's for a woman. It comes from the Chanvrerie Street barricade."

"If it's for Miss Cosette, I'll give it to her."

Gavroche agreed and ran off. Valjean went inside with Marius's letter and read it quickly. "The man that I hate is going to die, without me doing anything," thought Valjean. "I just have to keep this letter and Cosette will never know anything about it. But I must go to Chanvrerie Street to be sure."

———

That night, while the soldiers were sleeping, Courfeyrac and his men made the barricade bigger. When they were finished, Marius sat with his head in his hands, waiting for the attack in the morning. Then, he heard a noise and looked up. Cosette's father, Monsieur Fauchelevent, was there. He did not understand how this was possible, but everything felt like a dream to him now.

"Who is this man?" asked Courfeyrac.

"I know him," said Marius. But Monsieur Fauchelevent did not look at him.

"Then welcome," said Courfeyrac. "You know that we're all going to die?"

Javert also looked up and stared at Valjean.

Courfeyrac and his men did not have much longer to wait. Soon, a terrible noise could be heard along the street.

"They're bringing a cannon!" said Courfeyrac.

At the same time, Gavroche appeared.

Marius hurried towards him. "Why are you here? Did you deliver my letter?"

"Of course," said Gavroche.

But Marius was worried that the boy was back. He was hoping to keep Gavroche safe.

"They have a cannon!" said Gavroche. "We can fight back, but we need more bullets!" He climbed over the barricade, and began to pick up bullets from the dead soldiers.

"Come back!" shouted Courfeyrac. "You'll be shot!" And, at that moment, the soldiers began to fire.

"I don't care if it's raining," replied Gavroche, laughing. And he jumped down to the street and ran towards more bodies. The air was filled with smoke and for a while Gavroche was **hidden** as he went from one body to the next. As he moved away, the smoke began to lift. A bullet hit the dead body next to him. Another bullet hit the ground. Gavroche looked up, straight into the eyes of a soldier who was pointing a gun at him. The little boy began to sing as

he picked up the bullets. Suddenly, a bullet hit him and he fell. Then, he sat up and continued to sing. A second bullet hit him and this time he did not get up.

Marius ran to Gavroche, but it was too late. He was dead. Marius picked up the child and carried him into the inn, not noticing the soldiers firing at him. "Thénardier brought back my father alive," Marius thought, "but I'm bringing his child back dead."

"There's blood on your head," Courfeyrac said when he entered the inn. "You've been hurt." But Marius did not care.

"The end is coming," Courfeyrac told his men. "And we'll fight to the end." Then, he turned to Javert. "I haven't forgotten about you, spy. We don't want your dead body with ours. Someone will take you outside and shoot you."

"I'll do it," said Valjean.

Javert looked at him. "Of course," he said, quietly.

"Take the spy out the back," said Courfeyrac. "Everyone else, go out to the barricade!"

Valjean untied the ropes round Javert's feet and the policeman stood up. Then, with a gun in his hand, Valjean took Javert outside. Marius watched them go.

Valjean stopped in a dark corner, put down his gun and got out a knife.

"You're going to use a knife, not a gun," said Javert. "Yes, that is like you."

Valjean said nothing. He cut the rope round Javert's chest and hands, then he said, "Go."

Javert stared at him.

"I don't think that I'll get out of here alive," Valjean continued. "But, if I do, my address is 7 Homme-Armé Street."

Javert began to walk away. After a few steps, he turned and shouted, "I don't understand! Why didn't you kill me?"

"Go now," said Valjean.

Javert slowly walked away. After Javert was gone, Valjean pointed his gun at the sky and fired into the air. Then, he went back to the barricade and told Courfeyrac, "It is done."

Hearing the shot, Marius thought of his visit to Javert many months ago and his heart went cold.

A short while later, the last, terrifying attack on the barricade came. The cannon fired, bullets flew, and the noise was terrible. Courfeyrac was killed. Then, a bullet hit Marius's chest and he started to fall to the ground. But a strong hand took hold of him. "They're taking me prisoner, Cosette," was his last thought. "They will shoot me."

CHAPTER ELEVEN

Escape through the sewers

No one saw Valjean lift Marius up and carry him away from the barricade. But where could he go? There were high walls all around and only a bird could find a way out. Then, Valjean noticed a dark hole in the ground, with metal bars over it. He hurried towards it and found that he could lift up the bars. He put Marius on his back, not knowing if he was dead or alive, and climbed into the hole. It was not very deep and he soon found himself walking down a long path under the ground. It was totally dark and silent. He was in the **sewers** of Paris. He was safe!

Valjean walked and walked. When his path joined another, he chose to go uphill. "The river is at the bottom of the hill, and there'll be lots of people there," he thought.

Valjean kept walking. He was hungry and thirsty and he began to get tired. He stopped to rest and laid Marius down. The young man's eyes were closed and his hair and chest were wet with blood. Valjean took off his shirt and tied it round Marius's head. Then, he found Marius's notebook in his coat, with his grandfather's address. After this, he picked Marius up again and continued to walk. On and on he went, until he reached water. He could not go back so he walked through the water, which got deeper and deeper. Finally, on the other side of the water, he could see a light. It was a gate by the river. There was a way out.

But, when Valjean reached the gate, he found that it was locked. He put Marius down and dropped to his knees. It was impossible to go back. What now?

Suddenly, he heard a voice say, "If you give me half, I'll unlock the gate. I have the key."

"What do you mean?" asked Valjean. He looked at the man and saw that it was Thénardier.

"You've killed that man and you're going to steal his money. So give me half the money and I'll open the gate," said Thénardier.

"I haven't stolen anything," said Valjean. His face was so dirty that Thénardier did not know who he was.

As Thénardier looked in Marius's coat, he pulled a piece off it without Valjean seeing. "One day, it may prove who this man is," he thought. "There's only 30 francs here," he said to Valjean, taking all the coins. Then, he opened the gate very quietly, just enough for Valjean to carry Marius through. Thénardier locked it behind them and disappeared into the sewers.

Valjean was outside! He could see the sky and breathe the clean air again. But he soon had the feeling that he was not alone, and when he turned round someone was watching him. It was Javert.

"It's you!" Javert said. "I heard that Thénardier escaped from prison and I was following him. I was waiting for him to come out of the sewer, not you!"

"Javert, you've got me," Valjean said. "I am your prisoner. But I ask you one thing. Please help me carry this man home first."

"He was at the barricade, wasn't he? You've brought him from there?"

"Yes," replied Valjean. "I must take him to Monsieur Gillenormand, 6 Filles-du-Calvaire Street."

Javert agreed and together they laid Marius in Javert's carriage. They left Marius with the servant at his grandfather's house. Back in Javert's carriage, Valjean said, "Can we stop at my house for a moment? Then you can do anything that you like with me."

Valjean wanted to tell Cosette where Marius was and to say goodbye to her.

Javert did not argue and outside Valjean's house he said, "I'll wait here for you."

Valjean was surprised, but he hurried into the house. Cosette was not there. Then, he looked out of the window to the street. Javert was gone.

———

Javert walked along the river to a place where the water ran fast. His mind was full of confusing and terrifying thoughts. He understood good and evil, but he did not understand Valjean. "A convict gave me my life. A bad man did a good thing. How's that possible?" he thought. "My life has always been simple. Until now, I've always known what is right and what is wrong. I cannot bear this . . ."

Javert climbed on to the bridge and looked down into the dark water. He took off his hat and laid it on the wall. A moment later, he was standing on the wall. Suddenly, he jumped forward and fell into the darkness.

CHAPTER TWELVE
Darkness falls

For a long time, Marius's life was in danger, and his grandfather stayed by his bedside. Even as he got better, Marius could not remember much about the fighting at Chanvrerie Street and nothing at all about being carried away. But he hoped one day to find the man who saved his life, as Thénardier once saved his father.

After four months, Marius was finally out of danger, and only one thing filled his mind – to find Cosette.

"If I don't find her, I will die," Marius thought. But he was still sure that his grandfather would never agree to their marrying.

When Marius was almost strong again, he said to his grandfather, "I want to get married."

"Yes, you shall have the girl that you love," replied his grandfather. Marius stared at him. "You're surprised," continued the old man. "But while you were ill her father came here every day to ask about you. She's an angel, I hear. So get married and be happy." With that, the old man took Marius in his arms and began to cry.

———

It is impossible to describe how happy Marius and Cosette were when they finally met again. A date was soon agreed for their **wedding**. But Valjean knew that he could not lie about being Cosette's father at her wedding. He did not want things to be difficult for her, so he said, "Your real father was a cousin of mine called Fauchelevent, who died."

Valjean had another great surprise for Cosette. He gave her 600,000 francs as a wedding present. Before leaving Montreuil many years earlier, he hid the money in a box under the ground in the forest, together with the bishop's silver candlesticks. A few days before the wedding, he went to get the box from the forest.

On their wedding day, Marius and Cosette were the happiest people alive. But Valjean left early and went home alone. He took out the clothes that Cosette was wearing when he first met her carrying water in Montfermeil. He remembered walking away with her, hand in hand. "Maybe one day the darkness of my past will hurt her," he thought. "There can be no more lies." And he began to cry.

Very early the next morning, he went to speak to Marius. "My name isn't Fauchelevent. It's Jean Valjean," he said. "I was a convict for nineteen years. After I was released from prison, I stole again and I've been on the run from the police ever since. I mustn't continue to lie to you. To live, I once stole some bread. To live today, I will not steal a name. But please don't tell Cosette! A life without her is worse to me than death!"

"I won't," answered Marius, coldly.

"May I still visit her sometimes?" said Valjean.

"Come for a short visit at the end of each day," said Marius.

Marius was very surprised and unhappy. "Why did he have to tell me?" he thought. Then, he remembered Valjean escaping from the police at Thénardier's house. He remembered Valjean shooting Javert at the barricade. "He's not an honest man! Maybe he stole the money that he gave Cosette. I cannot use that money without knowing."

Valjean was miserable, too. His visits to Cosette became shorter and shorter, until one evening he did not come at all. He sent Cosette a message saying that he was busy. The next day, Valjean did not leave his room. The day after that, he did not leave his bed. He stopped eating. The doctor was called.

"He's very sick. He has lost someone dear to him. People can die of that," said the doctor.

That same day, Marius's servant brought him a note from a man named Thénard. Marius remembered Jondrette's handwriting from many months ago. "I have a secret to tell you," the note said. Marius knew that it was from Thénardier.

"Bring the man in," he told his servant.

Thénardier appeared and said, "Monsieur, your wife's father has stolen money. He's a murderer. His real name is Jean Valjean. If you give me 20,000 francs, I'll tell you more."

"I already know his real name and I also know yours," replied Marius. "You are Thénardier. You were an innkeeper in Montfermeil, you changed your name to Jondrette in Paris and you were my neighbour. But we never met.

I can tell you secrets about Valjean, too. He lived in Montreuil and I believe that he stole money from a factory owner there named Mayor Madeleine. I also know that he murdered the policeman Javert."

Thénardier looked surprised. "You have the wrong idea," he said. "Valjean *was* Mayor Madeleine of Montreuil. And he didn't kill Javert because Javert killed himself. The person that he stole from was a young man that he killed in the sewers. I saw him carrying the body with my own eyes. I can prove it by showing you a piece of the young man's coat."

Marius could not believe it. "That's from my coat!" he said, looking at the piece that Thénardier was showing him. "That young man was me! Now take this money, go to America and never come back!"

As soon as Thénardier was gone, Marius hurried to find Cosette. "Come quickly! We must visit your father. He was the one who saved my life!"

When Valjean heard the knock at his door, he was sitting at his table, writing a letter. The bishop's candlesticks were on the table.

Dearest Cosette,
Your husband is a good man – you must always love
him after I'm gone. I promise that the money which
I gave you is really your own. I once owned a factory
and I became rich. I also leave you my two silver
candlesticks . . .

He stopped, put his head in his hands and began to cry. Then, he heard the knock at the door and saw Cosette and Marius hurry in. Cosette ran into his arms.

"You're the angel that saved my life!" cried Marius. "Why did you hide it from us?"

"Because I thought that I should leave you," said Valjean, quietly.

"Never! You won't be here tomorrow!" said Marius. "We're taking you with us."

"It's true that I won't be here tomorrow, but I won't be at your house, either," said Valjean. "I'm going to die."

"No!" cried Cosette.

"It is nothing to die; it is terrible not to live," Valjean replied, his voice even quieter now. "Cosette, your mother's name was Fantine and she loved you very much. I'm going away, children. Love each other always. There's nothing more important in the world. I die happy."

Cosette and Marius fell to their knees, each holding one of Valjean's hands, and a great angel waited in the darkness to receive him.

During-reading questions

1 Why is it difficult for Valjean to find somewhere to stay?
2 What does Valjean steal from the bishop?
3 Why does Valjean try to find Petit-Gervais?

CHAPTER TWO

1 Why does Fantine leave her daughter with Madame Thénardier?
2 How did Mayor Madeleine become rich?
3 Why does Fantine sell her hair and her teeth?

CHAPTER THREE

1 Where did Javert first meet Mayor Madeleine?
2 What does Mayor Madeleine have to do in Arras?
3 Where is Valjean going at the end of the chapter and why?

CHAPTER FOUR

1 In what ways are the Thénardiers bad people?
2 What is Cosette doing when Valjean finds her?
3 Who is Valjean afraid of meeting in Paris?

CHAPTER FIVE

1 Why does Marius live with his grandfather?
2 What ideas do Courfeyrac and his friends talk about?
3 Who is Marius's "angel"?

CHAPTER SIX

1 What does Marius find on the ground near his building?
2 How can Marius see into his neighbours' room?
3 Who are the two visitors that Marius sees in the
   Jondrettes' room?

CHAPTER SEVEN

1 What does Javert want Marius to do?
2 Why does Jondrette's daughter sing a love song, do you think?
3 Why doesn't Marius fire the gun?

CHAPTER EIGHT

1 Why does Valjean want to hide from Marius?
2 How does Éponine stop Marius feeling so miserable?
3 Why do Marius and his grandfather argue again?

CHAPTER NINE

1 Who gives Marius a message in Plumet Street?
2 How does Éponine save Marius's life?
3 How does Marius plan to keep Little Gavroche safe?

CHAPTER TEN

1 Why does Valjean read the letter for Cosette, do you think?
2 How does Javert feel when he sees Valjean at the barricade, do you think?
3 Why does Valjean give Javert his address, do you think?

CHAPTER ELEVEN

1 How does Valjean escape from the barricade?
2 What does Thénardier take from Marius?

CHAPTER TWELVE

1 What does Valjean give Cosette as a wedding present?
2 Why does Marius think that Valjean is not an honest man?

After-reading questions

1 How does Valjean change after meeting the bishop?
2 Why does Fantine's life become so difficult?
3 Why does Javert kill himself, do you think?
4 Who is your favourite character in the story, and why?
5 There are many unusual families in the story. Which characters do not live with their real mothers or fathers, and why?
6 Why is the book called *Les Misérables*? Is it a good title, do you think?

Exercises

CHAPTERS ONE AND TWO

1 **Match the words together. Then write sentences about the story in your notebook.**
Example: 1 – *f*
Valjean was a convict who has just come out of prison.

1	convict	**a**	palace
2	bishop	**b**	hair
3	servant	**c**	inn
4	silver	**d**	francs
5	landlord	**e**	town
6	coins	**f**	prison
7	mayor	**g**	kitchen boy
8	barber	**h**	candlesticks

CHAPTER THREE

2 **Complete these sentences in your notebook, using the names from the box. You can use the names more than once.**

Javert	Valjean	Thénardier
Cosette	Fantine	Mayor Madeleine

1 Mayor Madeleine orders ...._Javert_...... to release ....
2 .... is very ill.
3 .... sends 600 francs to ....
4 .... believes that the real .... is in Arras.
5 .... cannot save .... if he is in prison.
6 At the trial, ... proves that he is the real ....

3 **Complete these sentences in your notebook with the correct form of the verb.**

1 Thénardier ...._was pulling_.... (**pull**) the ring from a dead soldier's finger when the man suddenly .... (**speak**).
2 "I .... (**carry**) that bucket for you," the man told Cosette.
3 "That's where I .... (**stay**) tonight," said the man.
4 "You .... (**be**) a long time!" shouted Madame Thénardier.
5 "If I .... (**take**) her, I .... (**not tell**) you my name," said the stranger.
6 Valjean changed direction to check that the .... (**not follow**).
7 A policeman .... (**hide**) in the darkness at the end of the street.
8 It was Fauchelevent, the old man who .... (**fall**) under the cart years ago.

CHAPTER FIVE

4 **Put these sentences in the correct order in your notebook.**

    a .... Marius sees a beautiful young woman in the
              Luxembourg Gardens.

    b .... Courfeyrac invites Marius to live with him in Paris.

    c .... Georges Pontmercy dies.

    d .... The young woman and her father move house.

    e .... Marius follows the young woman home.

    f ..*1*... Georges Pontmercy fights at the Battle of Waterloo.

    g .... Marius argues with his grandfather.

    h .... Marius tries to find Thénardier.

5 **Correct these sentences in your notebook.**

    1 Marius lives in a beautiful building.
       Marius lives in a miserable building.

    2 Jondrette tells his daughters to write letters for him.

    3 Before the old man arrives, Jondrette throws some wood on
       the fire.

    4 Jondrette's daughter cut her hand on a machine at work.

    5 Javert gives Marius 60 francs.

    6 Marius is standing on the chair when Jondrette's daughter
       comes into his room.

    7 The old man writes his address on the front of the letter.

    8 When the police arrive, the old man asks them for help.

CHAPTER EIGHT

6 Complete these sentences in your notebook, using the words from the box. Sometimes two answers are possible.

that	who	which	where	what	why	when

1 Thénardier was another person ......*that / who*......Valjean needed to hide from.
2 He hated this young stranger .... might take his dear child away.
3 There was a secret path between two high walls .... Valjean always used.
4 The only place that he liked to be was an empty field .... he could be alone.
5 He was here one morning in spring .... a young woman came towards him.
6 The next evening, without knowing .... , she put on her best dress.
7 "I don't want to leave you, but .... else can I do?"
8 "Does the girl .... you want to marry have money?"

CHAPTER NINE

7 Choose the correct word to complete these sentences in your notebook.

1 "The new *revolution* / **storm** is beginning!"
2 Marius **fired** / **shot** one of Javert's guns.
3 "I'll use this gunpowder to **blow up** / **shoot** the barricade!"
4 "We've already taken a **flag** / **spy**."
5 A man was **picked** / **tied** up with ropes near the wall.

CHAPTER TEN

8 **Put the words in the correct order to make questions.**
Then write the questions and answers in your notebook.

1 Valjean / where / sitting / was / ?
   Where was Valjean sitting? He was sitting outside his house.

2 letter / did / come / where / the / from / ?

3 did / night / men / during / what / and / Courfeyrac /
   his / do / the / ?

4 Gavroche / shot / was / when / doing / he / was / what / ?

5 Javert / taken / did / outside / why / Courfeyrac / to /
   want / be / ?

6 Marius / after / who / a / bullet / was / think / by / did /
   about / he / hit / ?

CHAPTERS ELEVEN AND TWELVE

9 **Write the opposites of these words in your notebook.**

1 lift up   *put / lay down*   6 wrong   ....

2 dead   ....   7 possible   ....

3 silent   ....   8 happiest   ....

4 lock   ....   9 worse   ....

5 evil   ....   10 life   ....

10 **Write the past simple of these verbs in your notebook.**

1 steal   *stole*   5 lie   ....

2 prove   ....   6 hide   ....

3 breathe   ....   7 release   ....

4 argue   ....   8 shoot   ....

Project work

1 Choose a character from the story and write about them using as many new words from the glossary as you can.

2 Imagine you are Fantine. Write one of her letters to the Thénardiers, when she sends them money (Chapter Two).

3 Choose one of these headlines and write the newspaper report:
- *Dangerous convict released from prison* (Chapter One)
- *Young boy shot at barricade* (Chapter Ten)
- *Policeman found dead in river* (Chapter Eleven)

4 Compare the book to a film of *Les Misérables*. How are they the same/different? Why did the writer make these changes for the film, do you think?

5 What happens to Marius and Cosette after the story, do you think? Write reasons for your answers.

An answer key for all questions and exercises can be found at
www.penguinreaders.co.uk

Glossary

angel (n.)
Angels live with God, wear white clothes and have wings. They are good and help people. In this story, *angel* is also used to describe a kind and beautiful person.

argue (v.)
when people talk to each other in an angry way because they do not agree

barricade (n.)
something that is built across a road, door, etc., to stop people from going past

beat (v.)
If your heart *beats*, it moves and makes the same sound again and again. When you are very excited or worried, your heart *beats* fast.

bishop (n.)
the most important priest (= a person who people listen to in church and who does *weddings*, etc.) in a city or part of a country

blood (n.)
Blood goes round your body and comes out if you cut your body. *Blood* is red.

blow up (phr. v.)
to break something suddenly with a loud noise and a lot of fire

breathe (v.)
1) to take air into and out of your body through your nose and mouth
2) to say something very quietly

bullet (n.)
a small piece of metal that comes out of a gun very fast and can hurt or kill someone

calm (adj.); **calmly** (adv.)
A *calm* person is not angry, frightened or worried. *Calmly* is the adverb of *calm*.

confusing (adj.)
difficult to understand

convent (n.)
a building where *nuns* live and work

convict (n.)
someone who is in prison because they have done something that is against the law (= the right and wrong things to do in a country)

darkness (n.)
when there is no light or almost no light

deliver (v.)
to take something like a letter, etc., to a person or place

director (n.)
a person who has the most important job in a hospital, school, factory, etc.

evil (n.)
Evil is very bad and horrible. Bad things happen because of *evil*.

faint (n.)
when someone suddenly falls to the ground because they are frightened, ill, too hot or have had a very big surprise

fire (v.)
You *fire* a gun when you use it.

gunpowder (n.)
a special powder (= something like sand that is soft and dry) that is used to *blow* things *up*

hide (v.); **hidden** (adj.)
past tense: **hid**
1) You *hide* in a place because you do not want people to find or see you.
2) You *hide* something because you do not want people to find or see it. *Hidden* is the adjective of *hide*.

honest (adj.)
An *honest* person says what is true and does not lie, steal or do bad things to people.

inn (n.)
a small hotel. People often buy drinks or food there.

jewellery (n.)
beautiful things that you wear on your neck or hands, like rings, etc., often made of *silver* or gold (= an expensive bright yellow metal).

landlord (n.)
a man who owns or manages an *inn*

lift (v.)
to move someone or something up

lock (v.)
If you *lock* a door, gate, etc., you close it with a key because you do not want people to open it.

mayor (n.)
the most important person in a town's or city's government (= a group of people who decide what must happen in a place)

miserable (adj.); **misery** (n.);
miserably (adv.)
If you are *miserable* or in *misery*, you are very unhappy. *Misery* is when you feel *miserable*, or is a thing that makes you *miserable*. *Miserably* is the adverb of *miserable*.

nun (n.)
a woman who is part of a religious (= following a way of believing in God) group of women that live together

palace (n.)
a very big, beautiful house. It is often the home of an important person like a king, queen or *bishop*.

prove (v.)
to show that something is true

release (v.)
to let someone leave a prison or other place where they were kept

revolution (n.);
revolutionaries (n.)
when people try to change the government or *ruler* of their country by fighting against them. These people are *revolutionaries*.

ruler (n.)
a very important person who says what must happen in a country

servant (n.)
A *servant's* job is to cook, clean or do other work in someone's home.

sewers (n.)
a group of very big pipes (= long, round things that air or water can move through) under the ground. They carry away things like dirty water or people's waste (= what comes out of a person's body when they use the toilet).

shoot (v.)
past tense: **shot**
to use a gun because you want to hurt or kill someone

silver (adj. and n.)
Silver is a bright grey/white metal that is used for making *jewellery*, money, etc. *Silver* things are made of *silver* or are the colour of *silver*. *Silver* also means beautiful things that are made of *silver*.

simply (adv.); **simple** (adj.)
If you live *simply* or have a *simple* life, home, etc., you have only what you need and nothing else.

spy (n.)
A *spy* tries to learn secret things another person, a group of people or a country.

stare (v.)
to look at someone or something for a long time

stranger (n.)
a person who you do not know

terrifying (adj.); **terrified** (adj.)
A thing or person that is *terrifying* makes you very frightened. You are *terrified*.

tie (v.)
to put a rope round something or someone. You *tie* the ends because you do not want that thing or person to move.

wedding (n.)
Two people get married at a *wedding*.